DESERT GIANT

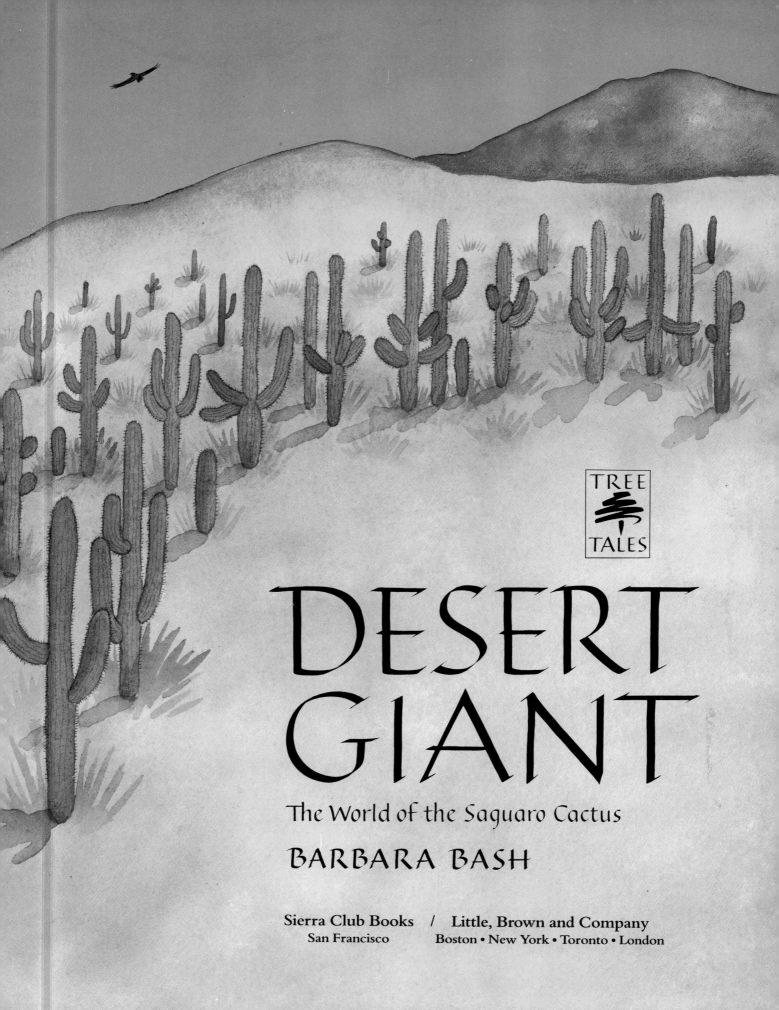

TREE
TALES

DESERT
GIANT

The World of the Saguaro Cactus

BARBARA BASH

Sierra Club Books / **Little, Brown and Company**
San Francisco · Boston • New York • Toronto • London

To Audrey Benedict, who first led me out into the desert,
and the Tohono O'odham Indians (the Desert People),
who live in the saguaro world

The Sierra Club, founded in 1892 by John Muir, has devoted itself to the study
and protection of the earth's scenic and ecological resources—mountains, wetlands,
woodlands, wild shores and rivers, deserts and plains. The publishing program of
the Sierra Club offers books to the public as a nonprofit educational service in the
hope that they may enlarge the public's understanding of the Club's basic concerns.
The Sierra Club has some sixty chapters in the United States and in Canada. For
information about how you may participate in its programs to preserve wilderness
and the quality of life, please address inquiries to Sierra Club, 730 Polk Street,
San Francisco, CA 94109.

All calligraphy by Barbara Bash

Library of Congress Cataloging-in-Publication Data

Bash, Barbara.
    Desert giant: the world of the saguaro cactus/by Barbara Bash.
  —1st ed.
     p.   cm.
    Summary: Documents the life cycle and ecosystem of the giant
  saguaro cactus and the desert animals it helps to support.
    ISBN 0-316-08301-1 (hc)
    ISBN 0-316-08307-0 (pb)
  1. Saguaro—Juvenile literature.   2. Saguaro—Ecology—Juvenile
literature.   3. Desert ecology—Juvenile literature.   4. Botany—
Ecology—Juvenile literature. [1. Saguaro.   2. Cactus.
3. Desert ecology.   4. Ecology.]   1. Title.
QK495.C11B32 1989
583'.47—dc19   88-4706
                                                   CIP
                                                   AC

Sierra Club Books/Little, Brown children's books are published by Little, Brown
and Company (Inc.) in association with Sierra Club Books.

HC: 10 9 8 7 6
PB: 10 9 8 7

HOR

Published simultaneously in Canada by Little, Brown & Company
(Canada) Limited

Printed in the United States of America

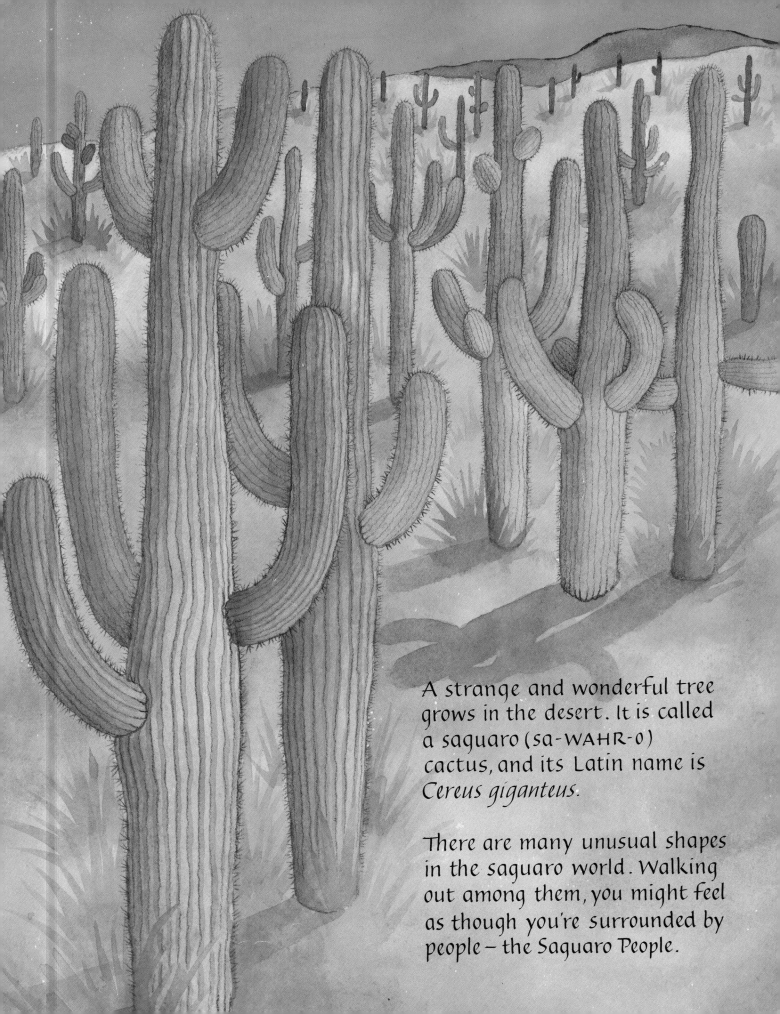

A strange and wonderful tree
grows in the desert. It is called
a saguaro (sa-WAHR-o)
cactus, and its Latin name is
Cereus giganteus.

There are many unusual shapes
in the saguaro world. Walking
out among them, you might feel
as though you're surrounded by
people – the Saguaro People.

The saguaro grows in the Sonoran desert, which stretches through parts of Arizona, California, and Mexico. This cactus can grow as tall as fifty feet, weigh up to several tons, and live for two hundred years.

The saguaro's sharp spines protect it from harm. The accordion-like pleats in its skin expand in the rain, storing extra water for the long dry times.

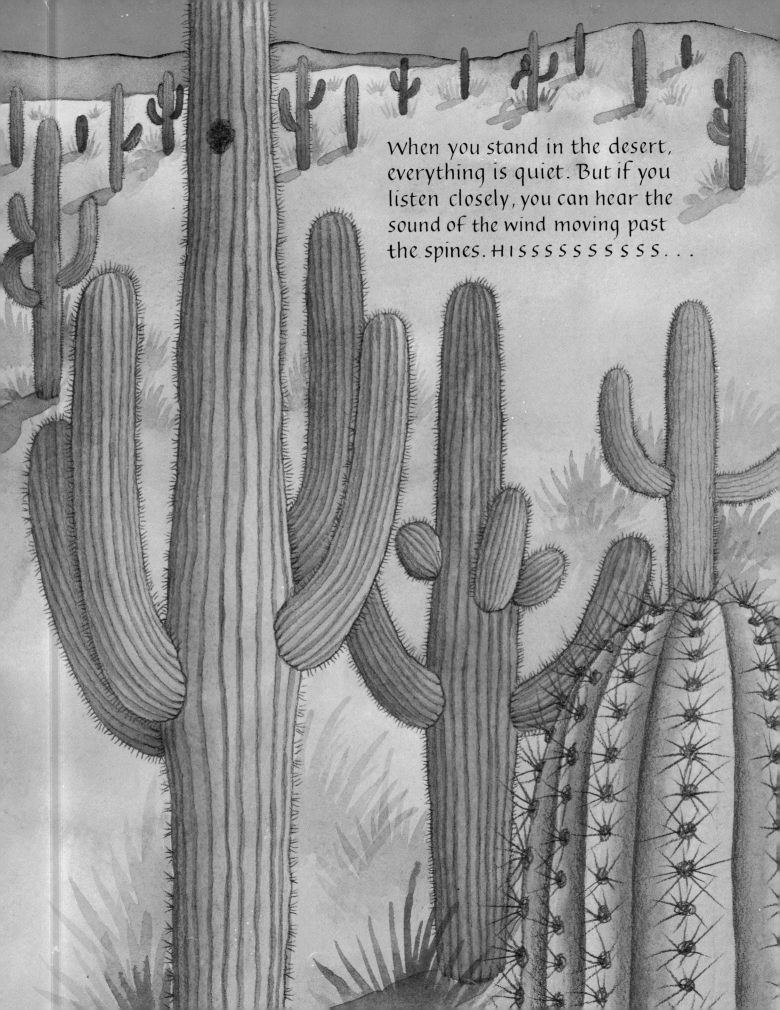

When you stand in the desert, everything is quiet. But if you listen closely, you can hear the sound of the wind moving past the spines. HISSSSSSSSS...

Now there is another sound: tap...
tap-tap...The holes you see in the
saguaro trunk are made by the
"carpenter bird"— the Gila (HEE-la)
woodpecker. In the spring, the male
pecks deeply into the soft flesh of
the cactus to make a room for
his mate's eggs to hatch.

The saguaro flesh forms
a hard, callous lining
around the nests. When
the cactus dies and
decomposes, these
hollow forms are left
behind on the ground.
They are called "saguaro
boots" by the Indians,
who use them as food
containers.

Male

Saguaro boot

Female

When the Gila woodpecker moves
out of its nest, the elf owl moves in.
This is the tiniest owl in the world,
measuring just five inches long.
The elf owl is nocturnal, hunting
for small insects, centipedes, and
scorpions at night and sleeping in
the nest during the day. Because
of the thick lining and the
moisture stored in the saguaro's
flesh, the nest stays cool even on
the hottest days.

Harris' hawks are the largest birds
to make their homes in the saguaro.
They raise their young in nests of
twigs lined with leaves and grasses.
Living in cooperative societies, much
like wolves, up to four hawks can
inhabit the same territory.

Sometimes the hawks use each
other as perches. As many as
three birds have been seen stacked
on top of a saguaro! This is called
Back Standing.

Back Standing

Nighttime. The moon shines in the dark sky. It is May, time for the saguaro to blossom. Out of the top of the cactus, high above the ground, the buds emerge and open into large, milky-white flowers with yellow centers. Each flower opens only once, in the cool of the night, and closes by the following afternoon.

Suddenly you hear a flapping of wings. A long-nosed bat has come to drink the nectar hidden deep in the center of the flower. As the bat drinks, the pollen dust sticks to its face and is carried along to pollinate the next bloom.

The next morning the white-winged doves arrive. They like to drink the flower nectar, too. One lands on top of the saguaro and dunks its head way inside. A queen butterfly alights on a petal, and a bee circles around, buzzing. Every creature that drinks the nectar picks up more pollen and carries it on to fertilize the next flower. When the flower is fertilized, the fruit can begin to form.

Stamen—
the male part of the flower that produces the pollen

Stigma—
the female part that catches the pollen

Ovary—
the container for the eggs (the fruit will form here)

Style—
the slender tube that carries the pollen to the eggs

It is very hot out under the desert sun. By early afternoon, the flowers that opened the night before have closed, and the doves have flown into the shade to rest.

By June, the saguaro blossoms have dried into brown stalks, and fruit has formed from the bases. The seeds are ripening, and the fruit begins to split open, revealing its bright red insides.

Dried flower stalk

Developing seeds

Ripe fruit split open with seeds exposed

As they have been doing for centuries, the Tohono O'odham (toh-HO-no o-O-dahm) Indians begin the saguaro-fruit harvest. The young women and children go out into the desert with buckets and gathering poles made of saguaro ribs bound together. Wooden crosspieces are wired onto the top and middle, forming the prongs that pull the ripe fruit down.

The children try to catch the fruit as it falls. Sometimes they steal a taste of the sweet, juicy pulp.

As the fruit is knocked down, the women scoop the bright red pulp full of tiny black seeds into buckets. When the buckets are full and heavy, they are carried back to the camp.

The women leave the red outer hulls behind on the ground, open and facing up to the sky. This is the O'odham offering for rain.

At the campsite, the men gather wood for the fire, and the old women remove any pebbles from the fruit pulp. Then the pulp is mixed with water and cooked for a long time until it is thick and sweet. Finally, the cooked pulp is poured through wire mesh to separate the juice from the seeds.

The O'odham make jams and candies, syrups and wines out of the saguaro fruit. Harvest is a time of celebration because there is good saguaro food to eat and soon the rains will come.

Back at the saguaro, more fruit
is ripening. The curved-billed
thrasher comes to eat the
sweet pulp, and harvester ants
scurry around gathering the seeds.
The horned lizard waits by the
fallen fruit for the ants to walk by.
In a flash he catches one with his
long, fast, sticky tongue.

Nighttime. More fruit has dropped to the ground, and the air is cool. A coyote arrives to lick the fruit pulp out of the fallen rinds. Nearby, some javelina (hav-a-LEEN-a) pigs grunt and snort as they scoop up the sweet fruit.

It is a feasting time for the Indians, animals, birds, and ants. Everyone loves the saguaro fruit.

After providing food and homes for so many creatures, the saguaro eventually dies. Sometimes old age and weakening tissue make it prey to bacteria. The soft outer flesh falls away, exposing the saguaro ribs, which spread out like a big whisk broom. At other times, strong winds or lightning knock the saguaro to the ground, where it gradually decomposes.

Now a whole new set of creatures moves in to live in the saguaro. . . .

Inside the dead saguaro, termites chew the wood. A black widow spider spins her web. The giant desert centipede searches for insects. On top of a downed saguaro, a banded gecko basks in the sun, while underneath, a cactus mouse stores seeds in its cheek pouches and a spotted night snake curls in the cool darkness.

Deep inside, water is released as
the saguaro decomposes, and the
aquatic beetle swims through the
channels. A large hister beetle
probes the dark tunnels in search
of fly larvae and small insects.
The stripe-tailed scorpion looks for
prey amidst the rubble, while a
giant millipede searches for
decaying saguaro tissue to feed on.

While one saguaro dies, another begins its new life. Each fruit-bearing saguaro produces millions of seeds, but most are eaten before they can sprout. The seeds that do germinate grow so slowly that the tiny saguaros are easily knocked over by animals or washed away by flash floods.

The only saguaros that have a chance of survival are those that begin their growth in the shelter of a "nurse plant." The canopy of the larger tree protects the young saguaro, and for many years it grows safely. Eventually the nurse plant dies, but by then the saguaro is strong enough to stand alone. After fifty years, it begins to produce flowers and fruit. After seventy-five years, the saguaro's arms start to appear. . . .

Saguaro seeds

Four-month-old seedlings

Two years old

Twelve years old

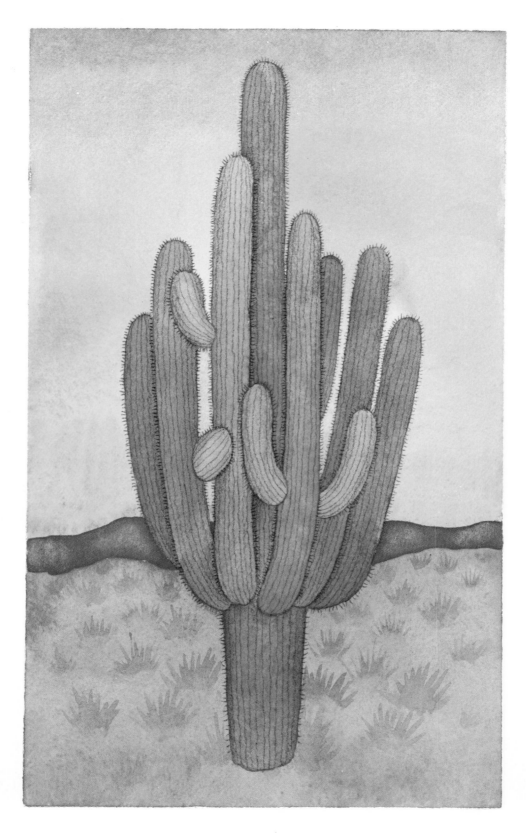

When it is one hundred fifty years old,
the cactus giant towers quietly
over the desert.